Janet Cassidy

Reading Advantage Authors
Laura Robb
James F. Baumann
Carol J. Fuhler
Joan Kindig

Project Manager
Ellen Sternhell

Editor
Jeri Cipriano

Design and Production
Preface, Inc.

Illustration
Bruce MacPherson

Printed in the United States of America

International Standard Book Number: 0-669-51404-7

2 3 4 5 6 7 8 9 10 - RRDC - 09 08 07 06 05

CONTENTS

CHAPTER

1

What's Going On?

Really, I never intended to be a hero. To look at me, Cyndi DeRello, you wouldn't expect me to be one, either. I'm all of five feet three inches tall. You would never think that I'd be the one to stand for Truth and Justice and fight against Evil by breaking up a ring of international dognappers. But I did!

It all started with Fran, my stepmother.

But let me backtrack and explain. Mom died four years ago, when I was ten. Eventually, Dad met Fran and as they say, the rest was history. They fell in love, they got married, and they started on the "Happily Ever After" part of their lives.

At least, *they* did. I was just along for the ride. Things actually weren't too bad at first. Fran would never replace my mom, but we got along okay.

There was just one little problem with the "Happy Ending," and that problem was Molly. Molly is my dog, a silly, little, mostly terrier mix that Dad gave me three years ago. She came along just when I was feeling too old to hug a teddy bear.

Fran, however, is just not a dog person. She thinks a dog belongs outside for sleeping. I think Molly belongs where she has always slept—at the foot of my bed.

Things came to a head in "Happily-Ever-After Land" when the new Prince was born. Prince Zack turned out to be a crying, colicky baby who is allergic to everything. But the number one thing that he is suspected of being allergic to is dog hair!

That's when Fran turned into the ES—the Evil Stepmother.

"Off with her head!" Fran shouted, pointing to Molly. (Okay, what she really said was, "Cyndi, I'm sorry, but we have to keep Molly away from the baby. She has to stay in your room or in the yard.")

Of course, I appealed to my father, the King, but it was no use. "Sorry, kid," he said. "Just listen to your stepmother on this for now, will you?"

I was insulted. Molly had been a member of the family long before Zack arrived. But now poor Molly was banished from the castle during the day. Little did I know then that her fate was almost far worse.

Now, during the day, Molly stays outside. Since our yard doesn't have a fence, Molly is kept on a chain attached to a clothesline that runs between two trees. This way she can get exercise. She has a doghouse in case it rains.

So it came to pass that on a Saturday morning two weeks ago, I was sitting on the front steps with Molly. I was waiting for Carrie and thinking about the unfairness of life. Caridad Diaz has been my Loyal Best Friend ever since fourth grade.

The first clue that Evil Was Around came while I was waiting. The messenger was Mrs. Oberholt, a woman who lives on our block. She was walking by when she spotted me.

"Cyndi, have you seen my Coco? She's missing from the yard." Coco was Mrs. Oberholt's poodle, a dog she doted on like a baby. She even had a wool coat and little boots for Coco to wear in the winter.

"You mean Coco ran away?"

"I don't know what to think. She has never run off before." Mrs. Oberholt sounded very worried. "I only left her for a few minutes."

"I'll keep an eye out for her," I promised.

The second messenger of Evil Tidings was Carrie. I spotted her mother's station wagon a few minutes later, following slowly behind a white van. I waved to Mrs. Diaz as Carrie jumped out of the car.

"Hi, Cyndi," said Carrie. Then she asked, "Why do you have such a long face?"

I told Carrie the latest complaint about my stepmom and she offered sympathy. Then she suddenly said, "Hey, I just remembered! Did you hear that Will McIntyre's dog, Sirius, is missing?"

Will McIntyre is my current idea of Prince Charming. He's in my science class. He is a nut for astronomy. That's why he named his dog Sirius—after the Dog Star. I think astronomy is pretty cool, too, so we do have that in common.

The problem is, Will doesn't know that he is a main character in my own personal "Happily Ever After" story. In fact, I'm not sure he even knows that I'm alive, but I had hopes of changing that.

"Will left Sirius in the yard when he went to school Thursday morning," Carrie explained. "When Will got home, the dog was gone!"

"Did he call the dog pound?"

"Sure. At first, Will thought that Sirius would turn up on his own. But Sirius still hasn't come home."

At the time, I wasn't keeping track, but that made two.

Number three was Molly.

CHAPTER

2

Where's Molly?

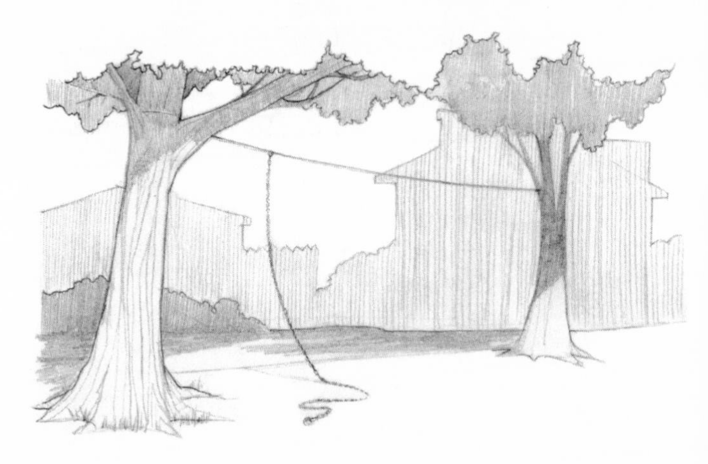

As I said, it started with Fran, my Evil Stepmother. She banished Molly from the family castle. I tried to explain to Molly why she couldn't sleep on the sofa during the day as she used to.

"I'm sorry, girl," I told her. "I know you don't understand, but it's all for the sake of the Royal Prince."

Each morning, I would put Molly on the run and make sure she had water. Then I would hug her tight. "Be a good girl. See you later," I would tell her.

But things went all wrong on Monday. The first thing I heard was Fran yelling, "Cyndi! Get up! You'll be late!"

I awoke and looked at the clock. Holy smoke! It was almost 6:30! If I didn't hurry, I would miss the bus. My first class was English, and if anyone was even three seconds late without an ironclad excuse, Mrs. Farley would deduct points. My English grade was already in the danger zone.

I leaped out of bed, dressed in a flash, and ran downstairs to put Molly on the run. Then I grabbed my backpack and jacket and sprinted the two blocks to the bus stop. I made a mental promise to make it up to Molly when I got home.

I got to the corner just as the bus appeared. I jumped on quickly and fell into the seat that my Loyal Best Friend had saved for me.

"I should be on the track team!" I panted. "I think I just set a record."

"I can see it now," said Carrie. "A new Olympic event—the Morning Bus Sprint with Heavy Backpack."

I was looking out the bus window and I saw a woman walking a black dog. It reminded me of Sirius. "I wonder if Will found his dog yet?"

Carrie smiled. "If he hasn't, you can offer sympathy and comfort him in his time of need."

Actually, I had something like that in mind. Alas, it was not to be.

The day that started off so badly got worse. In English, Mrs. Farley decided to give a pop quiz that I probably flunked. Mr. Ramos gave back the math quizzes from last Friday. I got a C minus. Carrie got an A.

I had looked forward to science class all day. It is usually the highlight of the day—one, because I like it, and two, because Will McIntyre is in my class. This was going to be my big chance to say more than "hi" to him. I was totally depressed when I found out Will wasn't even in school.

I was never so glad to see the end of a day. But the day was about to get much worse.

Carrie came home with me to help me with math. I let us in with my key and we headed to the kitchen. "Just let me check on Molly," I said, "and then I'll make us a snack." I was surprised Molly wasn't barking as she usually does when I get in.

"Where's your stepmom today?" Carrie asked.

"She took the Little Prince to the allergist," I answered, as I opened the back door.

Right away, I knew something was wrong. Molly was not on her chain. "Molly? Molly, where are you?" I shouted.

I dashed to the doghouse and got down on my hands and knees. I pushed aside the curtain that kept the cold air out. Molly was gone!

CHAPTER

3

Missing!

"Molly is gone!" I didn't get it. Where could she be?

Molly's chain lay on the ground, one end still fastened to the clothesline. I had this dreadful feeling in my chest.

"Maybe the chain broke and she got loose," said Carrie. That certainly was a reasonable conclusion.

I shook my head, starting to feel panicky. "It has a safety latch, so you can't just pull the chain free." I reached into the doghouse and felt Molly's dog bed. "It's warm! She hasn't been gone long!"

"Maybe your stepmother took her," said Carrie. "Maybe Molly got sick and your stepmother took her to the vet."

Or, I thought, maybe she decided it was time to just get rid of Molly. But Fran wouldn't do that, would she?

"I think she would have left a note," I said. I dashed back into the house to look with Carrie following me. I hadn't seen a note anywhere, but maybe I had missed it. I checked the usual places where Fran left notes, but I found nothing.

We both ran back outside to the front of the house, calling Molly's name.

"You go up the block," suggested Carrie. "I'll go this way."

We headed off to search the neighborhood. *Molly could not have gone far,* I told myself. *I'll find her. I have to find her!* I was fighting back panic. But I had a terrible thought. *What if Molly is missing just like Sirius and Mrs. Oberholt's poodle? What if I don't find her?*

Carrie and I searched the entire neighborhood for nearly two hours, checking every backyard and every patch of woods. We asked everyone we met, and we called and called, but no Molly. I even started looking in the street along the gutter, thinking that a car might have hit Molly. But she had simply vanished.

On Broad Street, we met Will McIntyre, who was stapling flyers with a picture of Sirius to all the poles. I was too worried about Molly to feel shy around him, the way I usually do.

When he heard about Molly, he was sympathetic. "I hope you find her. I have tried everything," he said. "I've been down to the pound three times. I put an ad in the paper, and then I made up these flyers."

"I guess I'll make flyers, too," I said. I was not encouraged by Will's news.

Will shook his head sadly. "It's as if Sirius just vanished off the face of the earth. It's funny, but Mr. Polaski across the street lost his dog the same way, the day before Sirius disappeared. He thinks his dog was stolen."

"Was his dog special?" asked Carrie.

"No," said Will. "Neither was Sirius, except to me."

"Hey," I said, remembering. "My neighbor's dog is missing, too! That makes four in a week! What's going on?"

"It's weird," said Will. "Who would steal dogs?"

"I need to call the pound," I said. "Molly had her license and tags on her collar. Maybe someone found her."

The pound was closed by the time we got home, so I left a message on their answering machine. Meanwhile, Fran and Zack came home from the allergist.

"Fran, have you seen Molly?" I asked. "She's not in the yard. I can't find her anywhere!" I held my breath. Would Fran say that she had taken my dog?

"No, I haven't, Cyndi," she said, looking concerned. "Are you sure she's not there?"

I wanted to say, "How could I make a mistake like that?" But at least Fran hadn't said she had taken Molly away.

"We've looked everywhere," I said, miserably.

"Mrs. DeRello," asked Carrie, "what time did you leave for the doctor?"

"Just before three."

"Was Molly in the yard then?" Carrie asked.

"I'm not sure," Fran said, thinking. "I know she was there earlier because she was barking at something. I had to go out twice to shush her."

"We got here just a little after three," said Carrie, "and her dog bed was still warm."

"She must have run off just after that!" said Fran.

"No, you don't understand," I said. "She couldn't get off her chain, and she wouldn't just run off, anyway!"

"But Cyndi, what else could it be?" asked Fran. "You don't think someone would take her, do you?"

I didn't want to think that. I only knew I had to find Molly.

Just as Mrs. Diaz arrived to pick up Carrie, Dad came home and I told him what happened.

"Come on," he said immediately. "We'll drive around and look for her. She may have chased after something and gotten herself lost."

I got my jacket and followed Dad to the car. We drove slowly up and down the streets, while I called Molly's name over and over. But, finally, we had to admit defeat and head home.

"We won't give up," my dad said. "We'll find

her." He gave me a hug as we walked to the house, which made me feel better. Sometimes I think I'll be lucky if I find a Prince Charming as good as my dad.

Fran had kept our supper warm, but I just wasn't hungry. I kept thinking of what Will had said. "Will's neighbor thinks his dog was stolen. Do you think someone would steal Molly?"

"I think it is more likely that Molly got loose and took off after a cat," suggested Fran. "I bet she'll come back on her own. Don't you think so, Josh?"

"Could be," said Dad. He put down his fork. He looked pretty serious. "Cyndi, I didn't want to mention this because I could be all wrong."

"Tell me, Dad." I had to know.

"I heard about some similar incidents last month, up in Franklinville, just north of here on the Canadian border," said Dad. "Seems there was a rash of dog disappearances up there, too."

"But why?" I asked. "I still don't see why anyone would steal dogs unless they have pedigrees, and then wouldn't they ask for a ransom?"

Dad hesitated. "Well, the police up north thought that the dognappers were stealing dogs and selling them to labs."

"To labs!" said Fran, horrified. "That's awful!"

Suddenly, I got the picture. "You mean for experiments? Oh, Dad, no! We can't let that happen to Molly! We've got to find her!"

Dad spoke calmly. "Now, we don't know that for sure. I may be all wrong."

"Let's call the police! Please, Dad!"

"Cyndi, we don't have much to go on."

"But maybe they can help," I begged.

Dad dialed the police station. He talked to a detective for a few minutes. When he hung up the phone, he said, "They promised to keep their eyes open. But the detective said that if it is dognappers, they don't stay in one town for very long. So it's extremely difficult to catch them in the act."

My heart sank.

Dad said, "There is something positive we can do tonight. Let's make up a flyer about Molly. We'll offer a reward."

He was right—at least it was something positive to do. But I didn't have much hope. A flyer hadn't helped Will get Sirius back.

CHAPTER 4

Dognappers

I hardly slept that night. I tossed and turned. Yet I had a dream, too. I kept hearing Molly barking. I followed the sound, but I couldn't find her.

When the alarm went off at 6:00 AM, my first thought was of Molly. Maybe she had come back home!

I raced downstairs in my bare feet. Maybe right this minute Molly was sitting outside on the back steps, wanting to be let in!

But she wasn't there. Molly was gone.

My feet and my heart both felt like lead as I went back upstairs and got ready for school. I wanted to cry, but I wasn't going to give up. I would find her somehow!

"Is she back?" asked Carrie on the bus.

I just shook my head, too depressed even to speak or think about it.

"We'll look for her after school," Carrie promised, "and we'll put up those flyers you made."

In science class, Mr. Jenkins was talking about the eclipse of the moon this weekend. When he gave a short break, Will came over. "Did Molly come back?" he asked. I shook my head.

"Sirius is still missing, too," Will said softly.

I told him about Dad's conversation with the police. "He thinks that maybe it's some dognappers who steal dogs and sell them to labs."

Will looked upset. "I would rather think Sirius got hit by a car," he said miserably.

I knew what he meant. I felt the same way.

After school, Carrie and I went to my house to get the flyers and a stapler. We headed down the block, stapling flyers to every pole. All the while, we kept our eyes open for Molly and kept calling her name.

For the next hour, we walked all over town and put up nearly fifty flyers. Finally, we sat down to rest on a bench in a park on Bartlett Avenue, five blocks from my house.

It was a quiet street, a nicer neighborhood than mine. While we rested, we watched the cars going by. Then Carrie remarked, "Did you see that van? That's the third time it has circled the block."

I shrugged. "Maybe the people in the van are looking for an address."

Then Carrie said, "Hey! I think I have seen that van before! It looks like the one my mother almost hit the other day."

When I looked puzzled, she said, "It was when she was dropping me off at your house. A van pulled out right in front of us and Mom had to slam on the brakes not to hit it."

"How rude!" I said.

"Then, it went about five miles an hour, and we were practically crawling along behind it."

As we were talking, a car pulled out of a driveway next to a two-story brick house. At the same time, the van came around the block again. It pulled over and parked just down from the house. It sat with its motor running for a few minutes.

"That *is* the same van," said Carrie. "I recognize the scrape in the paint on the back door."

"It's probably making a delivery," I said.

Just then, a man got out on the passenger side. He was short and wiry and wore a blue baseball cap, and he had something under his arm—a blanket or a towel. He looked around carefully.

"He doesn't look like a delivery man," I said.

The man didn't notice us. After a few minutes, he walked down the driveway of the house.

Carrie and I exchanged glances.

In a minute, we heard a dog barking from behind the house, and then all of a sudden, it was quiet. Then, as we watched, the man came hurrying back toward the street.

"He's got something in that blanket!" I said.

In the meantime, the driver of the van had hopped out and opened the back door of the van.

We were on our feet by now. When he opened

the door of the van, I caught a glimpse of something metal in the back. It looked like a cage! The man in the blue cap put whatever was wrapped in the towel into the back and slammed the doors. Then the two men jumped into the van and drove off.

We dashed out to the street. "Did you see that?" said Carrie. "They stole something from that house!"

"Get the plate number," I shouted as I ran toward the house.

"479—" shouted Carrie. "Oh, rats, it's too far away now."

I ran down the driveway of the house. Carrie followed me into the backyard.

"No doghouse," said Carrie.

"No, but we heard a dog barking," I said, "and look!" There was a dog chain attached to a clothesline, but there was no dog on it.

"Those guys must be the dognappers!" exclaimed Carrie.

"Let's see if the owners are home," I said. We ran to the front door, but no one answered the bell.

"I bet the dognappers were watching the house until they saw that car leave," Carrie commented. "Then they knew the owners were gone."

Dognappers! Could we really have seen the dognappers in the act?

"We have to find that van!" I said. "Let's call the police. We have part of the license number."

We got home just as Dad was pulling into the driveway. Quickly, we told him what we had seen.

"There might be a simple explanation," Dad said, "but it's definitely worth a call."

"I hope they can trace the van," Carrie said.

"That must be how they stole Molly," I said. "They were watching the house until no one was home."

"Yes, 153 Bartlett Avenue," Dad was saying. Then he said "thank you" and hung up. "They're going to call the people who own that house to see if their dog is missing."

Then Fran surprised me by saying, "Maybe Carrie would like to stay for supper?" I gave her a grateful smile.

A little while later, the phone rang and Dad answered. He listened for a few minutes. "Yes, that's fine. They will be here," he said and hung up. "The police are sending someone over to talk to you."

I gulped. I never had to talk to the police before. I hoped we weren't sending them on a wild goose chase. But then I thought of Molly and knew we had to follow every lead.

About fifteen minutes later, two officers arrived in a patrol car and knocked at the door.

"I'm Detective Langley," one said. "We spoke to the people who live in that house on Bartlett Avenue. Their dog is missing from their backyard, all right. It certainly sounds like you witnessed a dognapping. Tell us exactly what you saw this afternoon."

Carrie and I described what we had seen.

"It was the same white van my mother was following the other day," said Carrie firmly. "I'm sure."

Detective Langley smiled at us. "You girls did very well. Not everyone is so observant."

"I only got part of the license," said Carrie, apologizing, "but I know it was a commercial plate."

"We will run that plate number," he said, "and we'll be in touch. But it may take us a while to find the van. If you think of anything else, please call us." He handed me a small, white card.

"But when do you think you'll find Molly?" I asked.

The detective hesitated and said, "Look, I know how you feel. I have a dog, too. But I don't want to get your hopes up. The longer this goes on, the less chance there is that you'll get your dog back. It may already be too late."

I felt like I had just been punched in the stomach. It may already be too late? No, it just can't be too late! I had to find Molly!

CHAPTER 5

The White Van

The next day in school, I could not pay attention. I kept thinking, *What if it was already too late for Molly? What if she had already been sold to a laboratory? What if at this very minute . . .*

I had to get a grip on myself. "Don't go there," I said to myself. "Just keep thinking positive."

Fortunately, there was a teachers' meeting in the afternoon, so we had early dismissal.

"Let's get our bikes," I suggested to Carrie. "We can cover more ground that way, and maybe we will see that van." Carrie promised that she would be over as soon as she could.

When I got home, Fran was giving the Little Prince a bottle in the living room. I sat down to watch him. When he wasn't squalling, he was really cute, this little brother of mine. "Why does he cry so much?" I asked.

"I wish I knew," said Fran. "He cries when he's hungry. But after I feed him, he still cries and spits everything up."

Suddenly, I noticed how tired Fran looked. I knew Zack wasn't sleeping well at night. This couldn't be easy, I realized. Fran must be exhausted as well as worried and frustrated.

"What did the doctor say?" I asked.

"She ran a lot of allergy tests. I'm waiting for her to call with the results."

"I hope you find out soon," I said.

Then Fran put her hand on my arm. "Cyndi, I'm really sorry about Molly's disappearance. I feel terrible about it, and I feel responsible."

"Thanks," I said. I could tell her concern was real. I *had* blamed her, but I knew it wasn't really her fault.

I told Fran about the plan to look for Molly.

"That's a good idea. If Molly did take off, she might have gotten pretty far. Don't forget your cell phone, and call me if you're going to be late."

"Okay," I agreed. It was a good idea to have the cell phone, I thought, as I slipped it into my pocket.

"Be careful," Fran added, "and if you see that van, call the police right away."

I planned to call the police, all right. But I knew if we found that van, I was going to try to follow it, no matter what. If there was any chance that Molly was still alive, I had to do everything I could to rescue her.

When Carrie arrived, we rode over to Bartlett Avenue and past the park we had sat in yesterday. We circled the block and then expanded our route, riding slowly up and down each block. For three hours, we rode around town, from neighborhood to neighborhood. There was no sign of Molly, nor was there any sign of the white van.

"Let's head over to Market Street," said Carrie after a while.

We headed for the business district. There were more cars and trucks there, but we rode around for another twenty minutes without seeing a white van.

"Let's stop a minute," said Carrie, finally. "I need something to drink!"

That sounded great to me. I was discouraged and thirsty. We locked our bikes in front of the Island Bodega and went in. Carrie bought two colas and some pretzels and we sat on the bench outside to watch the street. The cool drinks tasted great.

Then Carrie shouted, "Look—a white van!"

Suddenly, I wasn't tired anymore. We jumped up, leaving our half-finished drinks, and dashed out to the bikes. The van was already four blocks ahead on Market Street, heading up the hill.

"Quick!" I shouted. "After it!"

CHAPTER 6

Caught!

I fumbled with the chain and padlock, and then I jumped on my bike to follow Carrie, who was already halfway up the street.

We pedaled hard, trying to catch up to the van. We saw it make a right onto Hampton Avenue. At least the red lights were working with us, and traffic was moving slowly. We stayed a few cars behind it.

Hampton Avenue leads west to a kind of rundown section of town with factories and warehouses.

Suddenly, the van pulled into the left-hand lane with its turn signal on. We watched as the van made a left turn. I caught a glimpse of the license. Sure enough, it began with 479!

Carrie saw it, too. "That's it! That's the license, and I saw the paint scrape! It's the same van. Call the cops!"

I yelled back, "I can't stop now. We'll lose them! Let's see where the van is going!" I felt a surge of energy. Maybe the van would lead us right to Molly!

My heart was pounding as we waited until the van was a safe distance ahead. Then we made the turn and followed. We rode on the sidewalk so the driver wouldn't see us in the van's rearview mirror.

After about a mile, the van turned left onto a narrow street of rundown buildings. There was garbage and broken glass on the sidewalks, too. A street sign read Garden Street. *Some garden,* I thought.

"Watch out for flats," Carrie cautioned.

Just then, the van's right signal started blinking. We slowed down and kept out of sight. We stopped and watched from a distance as the van pulled into a driveway between two high brick walls. Across the driveway was a tall metal gate, locked with a padlock and chain.

Carrie grabbed my arm when she saw a short man wearing a blue baseball cap jump out of the van. We watched him open the lock and the gate.

"It's him!" I whispered. The van drove in, and the man locked the gate from the inside.

"Let's get closer," I said.

We put our bikes and helmets in the alley across from the driveway, leaning them against the wall.

We crossed the narrow street to the metal fence. The chain and lock had been passed through an opening in the fence, and it made a good peephole.

We looked. The driveway led into a parking area in front of a low brick building. A small sign over the door read "Adams Express." The van was parked in front with its back doors open. Inside the van were several large dog crates, and each held a dog! The dogs were excited, jumping up and down and barking.

A tall man with stringy blond hair was talking to Blue Cap. "I told you the stuff was wearing off. Make them be quiet or someone will hear them."

"Shut up, you mutts!" It was Blue Cap.

"Give those mutts a good dose this time," said the blond guy. "I can't stand this racket."

I couldn't believe what I saw next. Blue Cap poured something from a bottle onto a rag. One by one, he grabbed each dog and covered the dog's head with the rag. The dog struggled for a minute. Then it lay down and seemed to sleep.

It must be chloroform, I realized. I was horrified to think they had drugged Molly this way.

As we watched, the men took each dog from its cage and carried it into the building.

As Blue Cap lifted the last dog, he said, "This makes fifty. Call Adams and tell him we've got enough mutts to fill the laboratory's order."

"Well, just treat them carefully," said the blond man. "They're no good to us dead."

They were still here! My heart gave a leap. It wasn't too late. The dogs were still here, and the men wanted them alive! But that meant we had to act quickly.

The men disappeared into the building.

"We've got to get in there!" I said.

Carrie was not enthusiastic. "What can we do against those men? Let's call the police."

I was determined. "I will in a minute. I just want to take a look in that window. There has to be a way to get past this gate."

The wall was about eight feet tall. On the right, it continued down the length of the property and was topped with barbed wire.

But on the left side, I noticed it was close to the wall of the building next door. And right there, in the wall of the neighboring building, was a low window with a stone frame. The top of the frame stuck out, just enough for a foothold.

I put my left foot on the stone window frame. "Give me a boost," I said. Carrie pushed, and I made it to the top of the brick wall.

"Give me your hand," I said. Carrie was tall, but light, so she was able to pull herself up.

"If we get caught, we're dead," she said.

"Shhh!" I warned. I dropped down from the wall into the parking area, and Carrie followed.

There were no windows in the front of the building. But around to the side, we could see two dirty windows about three feet above the ground.

"Keep low," I said. We crept carefully around the building. I inched my way closer to the window.

"Can you see anything?" whispered Carrie.

"Not yet. Wait," I said. Carrie crowded closer to look over my shoulder.

"Looking for something, ladies?"

We both jumped at the voice and turned to see Blue Cap with the blond man behind him.

"Why did you follow us?" asked Blue Cap. He studied Carrie and me with narrowed eyes.

He looked mean. *If he could drug dogs,* I thought, *what would he do to us?*

I wasn't going to let him see how scared I was. "What did you do with those dogs?" I asked boldly.

"Dogs? Oh, a dog lover, eh?" Blue Cap said, half smiling. "Well, we're just dog breeders."

I should have kept my mouth shut. They might have just let us go. Instead, I said, "No, you're not. I think you stole those dogs."

Blue Cap stopped smiling. "Shut up!" he said. "You want to see what's in here? I'll show you." He grabbed us roughly and pushed us toward the door.

I tried to twist free, but his grip was too strong. He was hurting my arm. We were caught!

CHAPTER

7

Inside the Warehouse

I looked at my watch. Three hours had gone by. Dad would be home from work, and he and Fran would be frantic by now. I could have kicked myself for getting caught.

Carrie and I were sitting on the floor in the corner of the warehouse office. So far, the men hadn't tied us up. But there was only one door out of the room, and the two men were sitting between the door and us. Escape was not possible right now.

"What are we going to do with these two?" the blond man asked.

"I don't know yet," said Blue Cap.

"Just let us go," I said. I tried not to sound frightened, but I was.

"Sure, and have you dash to the cops?" snarled Blue Cap. "You already know too much."

"We won't say anything," pleaded Carrie.

"We'll take them with us," decided Blue Cap.

"No!" I screamed. We couldn't let them take us.

"Shut up," said Blue Cap.

I was fighting panic. So far, the men hadn't hurt us, but what would happen later?

The blond man was talking. "Hey, stealing dogs is one thing, but now you're talking kidnapping."

I could feel the weight of my cell phone in my jacket pocket. If only I had called the police when we had the chance!

"Ahh, we won't hurt them much," Blue Cap said, grinning. "We'll let them go when we're a safe distance away."

I slipped my hand into my pocket and touched my cell phone. If only I could sneak a call without them hearing me.

Text! Maybe I could *text* message! But where were we? I racked my brains trying to remember the name of the last street we had turned onto.

"Look," said the blond man. "When Adams gets here with the truck, we load the dogs and get the heck out of here. Forget the kids. By the time they get out of here and find a phone to call anyone, we'll be long gone."

Adams! I thought to myself. *That was what the sign over the building had said—Adams Express. And the street—what was the street?* Then I remembered. *Garden Street!*

I slipped the cell phone quietly out of my pocket. I caught Carrie's eye as I shifted position. Carrie caught on right away and rearranged herself slightly to block me from the men's view.

"H-e-l-p," I spelled. "G-a-r-d-e-n-s-t" and "A-d-a-m-s."

Then I hit our number and sent the message. Just in time, for just then Blue Cap got to his feet.

"You!" He pointed to me. I stopped breathing. Had he seen the cell phone?

"You come with me. We've got a half-hour before the truck gets here for the pickup. You're going to help me feed those mutts."

I slowly got to my feet, and Carrie shot me a frightened look. I didn't want us to be separated. Our best chance was to stay together! Besides, I didn't like Blue Cap and I didn't want to be alone with him.

"We'll both help," I said, "so it will go faster."

Carrie jumped up, trying to look cooperative.

Blue Cap considered. "All right. But don't think you can try anything. That knockout juice works on kids, too."

He led the way into another room, where there were several large bags of dry dog food and a sink. Then he opened the door into a large room and was met with a chorus of yaps and barks. There were several rows of cages on two levels, about fifty in all. Was Molly in one of them?

"Fill the food bowls and give them water," said Blue Cap, "and don't try anything funny. I'm right here watching."

He went back and stood guard by the door. I wanted to search the cages for Molly but not while Blue Cap was watching.

We started with the first row. Carrie opened each cage door, while I reached in with a scoop of food to fill the bowl.

Carrie started to close the latch on the first cage when a new idea hit me. *Why not just leave the cages unfastened?*

"Wait!" I whispered. I closed the door, but I left the latch unlocked. The cages were too far away for Blue Cap to notice, and the dogs were too busy eating. But a cage door would swing open the minute a dog pushed its weight against it.

We moved from cage to cage, working quickly down the row. There was still a lot of barking, but I kept calling softly, "Molly? Molly, where are you?"

Suddenly, I heard Molly yipping excitedly from a cage near the end of the row. Molly had heard me!

"Molly!" I kept my voice low. "I'm coming, girl!"

We worked our way down the row, leaving each cage door unlatched. Finally, we reached Molly. I wanted to scoop her up and hug her. I was so relieved to see she was all right. But Blue Cap was watching.

"Don't worry, girl. We'll get you out of here!" I said. Molly pushed against the door, but I kept it closed. "No, girl, not yet! *Sit. Stay.*"

Obediently, Molly sat and stopped pushing against the cage door.

Then I recognized Will's Labrador, Sirius, in the next cage. "We'll get you out, too, boy," I whispered. I fed him and left his cage unlatched. Just then, a dog on the bottom row discovered his cage door was open and pushed his way free!

"Hey!" Blue Cap yelled. "What are you doing? Get that dog!"

"Quick! Get the rest!" I said. Carrie and I tried to unlock as many cages as we could before Blue Cap reached me and yanked me away from the cage. We actually got to unlock them all.

"You little brat. I told you, no tricks!"

"Molly!" I yelled as I struggled to get away. "Jump, Molly!"

Molly didn't hesitate. She pushed against the cage door and it opened. She ran out and hurled herself through the air like Mighty Dog, landing square against Blue Cap's chest. He staggered backwards. I pulled and got free. By then, Molly had grabbed his pants leg and was holding on as only a terrier can do!

In the meantime, it was bedlam. The other dogs had started barking and jumping against the cage doors. In a minute, the room was a madhouse of barking, swirling dogs.

"Get him!" I yelled. Surely one or two of these dogs would know what that meant. Sure enough, two dogs obeyed me and grabbed Blue Cap's pants legs, while another jumped up and grabbed his sleeve.

"Get them off me!" Blue Cap screamed.

The blond guy heard the racket and ran into the room. When the dogs saw the open door, they made a mad dash for it, knocking him over.

"Come on, run for it!" I shouted. Carrie and I ran for the door with Molly leading the way.

"You're not getting out of here!" yelled Blue Cap. He and the blond guy had shaken off the dogs, mainly because the dogs were just concerned about getting out. Now, the dogs were only a few yards behind us.

Then I remembered the wall and the gate. Could we get over them in time? I reached the front door and pushed it open. Carrie and I burst out, followed by fifty barking dogs, exactly at the moment the metal gate opened.

"Hold it right there!" said a voice. "Police!"

CHAPTER

8

In the Stars

So that's how it came to pass that I, Cyndi DeRello, became a hero. Of course, Carrie was also a hero. Dog owners all over town could rejoice. Best of all, I had Molly back.

I sat on the sofa, next to Fran, with Molly at my feet. We were both relieved to be home.

"You saved the day," said Fran, smiling at me.

"I'm glad the police got there so fast," I said.

"The pound came to round up the dogs, and they'll keep them until the owners are located," said Dad. "But Cyndi, you know you took a terrible chance following that van."

"I know, I know. I'm sorry, Dad," I said. "But I couldn't take a chance on losing sight of them. I might have lost Molly!"

Molly looked up and whined.

Fran laughed. "She really is smart, isn't she?"

"Yes, and she was brave, too. You should have seen her attack the dognapper!"

Fran reached out a tentative hand and petted Molly. *Wow*, I thought. *That was a first!* What was even better was what Fran said next.

"Oh, Cyndi, I almost forgot. I have good news! The doctor's report says that Zack has food allergies. He's not allergic to Molly, after all."

"He's not? You mean—"

"Yes," proclaimed King Dad. "Molly is welcome anywhere in the house!"

"Oh, thank you. That's great!" I hugged them both. No more Banished Dog. No more Evil Stepmother!

One of the perks of being a hero was that the next day, Carrie and I got to miss our morning classes. We had to go down to the police station.

"We have a good case against these characters," Detective Langley told us. "They were stealing the dogs and selling them to a laboratory in Canada. Transporting stolen merchandise across the border makes this an international matter.

"Then there are the assault charges as well as holding you girls against your will. So, thanks to you, these men are facing long prison terms."

Of course, we had our fifteen minutes of fame at school when we got back. The local newspaper sent a reporter to interview us.

And things were definitely looking up with Prince Will, too.

"Hey, I got Sirius back this morning," he said. "I thought I'd never see him again, and—well, thanks."

I smiled. "I'm glad we found them all in time."

"I was thinking," said Will. "If you're not busy this weekend . . . I have this new telescope. We could check out that eclipse together." When I grinned, he added, "I'll bring Sirius. I think he and Molly are going to be friends, too."

I couldn't stop smiling. "Sure. It's in the stars!"